MW00946947

UPON THIS ROCK
The Magdalene Speaks

by

ROXANNE FAY

Katrine —
Many thanks
for your
kindness!
Roxanne Fay

Copyright © 2014 by Roxanne Fay. All rights reserved,
including performance rights. Please address performance
rights/licensing requests to roxanne@roxannefay.com.

Author's Note

I would like to extend my deepest gratitude to Ned Averill-Snell and to Heather Jones for their friendship, support and assistance, and to Reverend Emily Bell and Margaret Starbird for their patient encouragement.

Thanks to Peter Tush and the Dalí Museum, St. Petersburg, Florida.

Thanks to Bob Devin Jones and the Studio@620 (St. Petersburg) and Theatre Tampa Bay, whose generous grant assisted in the research and formulation of this book, as well as the play derived from its text (premiere May 27, 2014).

This work is for my mother, Sylvette, and my dad, Larry, who guide me here on earth, and for my father, Milton, who guides me from within.

I am grateful for this journey.

I hear his voice.

"Mary."

Eloi, Eloi—lama sabachthani!

Do I dream? I do not sleep. There are no dreams left to dream. Only quiet brightness at my core.

It is The All. It is The Truth. Truth as memory. Truth remembered and so re-lived anew.

Truth distilled down to its essence, thickening my blood and letting it slow.

Slow. To a halt. Warm, thick blood of memory. Softening my being. Dissolving my bones.

Leaving only The Knowing. And The Truth that will at last be fully told.

THE FAMILY AT BETHANY

I was tired.

Tired of being the second thought.

The thing that was remembered only after what was truly desired was either obtained or lost. Something to fill the secondary space at the periphery of the picture. It made me bitter and jealous. It also made me work much harder than the fortunate ones—the "firsts." To be of value.

To be important to someone.

It was, perhaps, a large part of why I so readily left to follow him. My family had selected a husband for me by the time I was walking. A deal had been made. That in itself made me secondary. My father obtained what he desired by the jointure of our families—more wealth and more influence. There was no need for a thought about Mary.

She was... sorted.

I was married at fourteen years old and moved into my husband's family home in Bethany. My husband was then sixteen. My father-in-law had no thought about me one way or the other—I was part of the deal.

But my mother-in-law was disappointed.

2 Fay

I was already older than most brides.

And I was not very pretty.

I liked my husband. At first, he was like a big brother. When we were alone together in our quarters, he would read to me or ask me to sing for him.

I missed him when he was gone during the day. He and his father often traveled into Jerusalem or Galilee for family business. Then I was alone.

I didn't really mind, but at times, it would make me sad. The days were slow to pass and seemed grey, like they could not take on enough light.

One day, I did notice another young boy in the yard near our quarters.

My husband and I lived away from the main house and I rarely went out.

I wanted only to do my daily chores and wait for my husband to return.

If I saw a servant—or worse, my mother-in-law—I would recede into shadow and wait for them to pass. This time, I called out to the boy.

I knew his face.

This was my husband's brother, Lazarus.

I remembered him from my wedding day. He was a year or two younger than me. So beautiful! Small and mild and smiling. He came right in and we began to chatter like old friends who had not seen one another in years.

He was so intelligent. So bright! He had begun to read and write, so now, when my husband was gone, Lazarus would read and I would sing for him until late in the day.

Brighter days now. I never saw his parents except on the Sabbath. It was my job to set out the candles. Sabbath was very grim in that house. Very rigid and unsmiling.

My husband always felt so far from me. At the men's table.

I sat next to my mother-in-law at the women's table.

The seconds.

Not every household had separate tables like this, but we did there.

My mother-in-law was a cold woman.

The only time I would catch her smiling was when Lazarus was near her. Then her eyes would lighten and she became softer somehow. My sister-in-law, Martha, was a happy girl. I liked her. But she stayed close to her mother. Every day. In the main part of the house.

And this was life.

Spending days with Lazarus.

Waiting.

For my husband to come home. To see Martha at Sabbath. To set out the candles. To sit at the secondary table, tolerated by my mother-in-law.

After some years of this sameness, my husband fell ill and died very quickly. I remember that I cried. I felt a loss. He had treated me with care from the very first day I met him—the day we were married. On our wedding night, I had no idea what was supposed to happen and even less idea how to make that happen. I resisted his advances. I cried for my mother. At first he was upset—did I not think myself fortunate to be married to him? I thought he wanted to hit me. But he saw my simple confusion and fear. Finally, he laughed out loud and hugged me hard.

He said we would wait a while. We would be married for the rest of our lives, so there was time enough. He slipped out into the garden and caught a small bird. A dove. In our bed, he cut the bird's throat with a sharp knife and let some of the blood drip on to the linens.

I was horrified.

"What have you done?"

He took me by the hand and we carried the tiny body to a dark corner of the yard where he prayed over the bird. We buried it there.

"This dove has blessed us with time. Come back inside and I will explain." Early in the morning, before light, he balled up the linens and took them to the main part of the house to appease his parents' expectations.

I never saw the linens again. Life in the household was busy. Time passed and my husband seemed content to wait for me—he never spoke of it. But his parents were becoming anxious for us to have a child. Our delay was making them look bad in town. My husband would smile at them and say the Lord would bring us a child when He willed it so, not the neighbors. He was kind. The night we finally came together as husband and wife—there was no blood. No pain. I felt as if I were expanding—becoming more than just myself—filling up with a luminous energy.

I felt safe.

I felt treasured.

One part of a whole. Not the second thought.

I did not know what would happen to me when he died.

My own father would not want me back—he had obtained what he desired in the match and he would not be able to barter me out a second time.

My new family did not want this reminder of their dead son with them, but Lazarus spoke to them on my behalf. They were fair-minded people.

Because I was their son's widow and because Lazarus and Martha pleaded for me, they did not turn me out—which, as I saw later, sealed my fate. I was relegated to the secondary house in the back of the property behind the gardens to live on my own, joining the family only at Sabbath.

At eighteen, I became an old woman. A widow.

Outcast inside my own household. Mostly isolated but for Lazarus' visits.

I would leap up to open the door when I heard him coming. We craved each other's company. We talked for hours, we laughed. I loved him dearly—so much more than my own brothers who had no doubt forgotten me all ready. Lazarus and I had a bond.

Secrets.

His aversion to women and his fascination with the boys in the marketplace. And he taught me to read and write.

The biggest secret of all. A dangerous secret.

A literate woman.

Years went by and Lazarus and I grew closer, eventually drawing sweet, happy Martha into our circle. They were my family. Even their parents came to accept my presence—like a benign but rather useless pet. I shared more meals with them. I moved into the main house. When they died, I wept with an honest grief.

Lazarus, Martha and I lived in the main house together. It was like a real life. We ate our meals, tended our chores, went to market, went to Temple. In town, I was vaguely aware of the sideways glances; the whispers that became sudden silences, as we passed, but I ignored them. I was happy and I wanted nothing to disturb that happiness. We were a family. We were blessed with good land, a nice house and money enough to enjoy living there.

But as the whispers grew louder and became audible words, I realized that our created family was of no interest to them—it was the blessings—the land, the home, the money that they were talking about. Whispers became rumors.

As the weight of the Roman Empire sat heavier and heavier on our city and on our backs, the resentment toward those who knew comfort grew sharp. We rarely ventured into market now, sending a servant to purchase our needs. We still dared to go to Temple. Lazarus would smile and say that God wanted us at Temple, not hiding at home.

"Surely, nothing bad can happen to us in God's house."

And we would make the walk to Jerusalem.

That smile.

I try to remember it to see it in my mind's eye. But the memory is faint now. Time is a strong acid— blurring the beauty and gentleness of all it touches.

THE FALLEN WOMAN

We went to Temple that day.

It was crowded and breathless in the center of the city. Lazarus went to the inner court where the men were allowed to worship and study.

I remained in the outer women's court with Martha. As we took our places, the other women moved away from us. During prayers, they turned their backs. As Martha and I looked questioningly at each other, we could hear a clamor rising, coming from the inner part of the Temple. Something invisible struck at me, deep within my chest.

I don't know why, but I told Martha to run.

Run home and bar the doors.

I tried to follow, but got only as far as the chamber door. There in the courtyard, I saw Lazarus. Held fast by men's hands. Afraid. The men yelled my name: "Mary of Bethany! Come forth! Come forth or Lazarus will pay your penalty." What did they mean?

I walked out toward the men.

"Why are you holding my brother?"

"Brother!" One scoffed—I recognized him. This was the man—this was the Temple priest—who had once come upon me in the marketplace. He had followed me and gestured me to go with him into a corner or the square—away from sight.

I thought he would be able to tell me why the people were so cold to my little family—that perhaps I should talk to him. He did not want to talk.

Pinning me against the wall, he kissed me hard on the mouth. I felt him against me—hard there, too. His hands grabbing at me through my garments. His breath sour and hot in my face. I bit his tongue until I tasted blood. He threw me against the wall and spat red spittle at me.

"Temptress," he hissed, "Whore!"

Then he was gone.

Now, he reappeared: "She does not live as Lazarus' sister, but as his concubine—tempting his drunken friends and giving her body to them of her own accord, her own appetite. She shared Lazarus' bed before the death of her husband. She is an adulteress. She has defiled our law and will pay the penalty."

The penalty. We all knew it well. It was the stuff of scary stories children told each other in the dark.

Death by stoning.

Stunned. No breath. No sound. My ears vibrating with the coursing of my own blood. My guts disappeared—a hole in my core—all at once cold as ice, hot and humming like a taut wire. I stared. Not able to move or cry out in protest. The earth moving so slowly—arms clutching me, dragging me to the center of the courtyard.

Men were going to do this.

Men I had traded with at market. Men who had been at table in my house. Men of the Temple. I tried to keep my mind from thinking about how much it was going to hurt.

Men everywhere. Familiar and unknown. And then—the first man.

He knelt in the dust to pick up a stone.

I was transfixed. There was no one in the world but him—everything else blotted from my view. This man looked at me.

And I could see that he hated me.

This stranger.

Hated me.

Meant me harm. In the next moment, my vision cleared and the crowd swam back into view. A hand reached out and touched this hateful stranger on the shoulder. Looking up, he immediately demurred, as if all the strength had run out of him.

He placed the rock in the outstretched hand.

A man stepped past the crowd directly to me.

He offered the rock in his open palm to the mob.

"I will give this rock to anyone among you can look in the face of God and say that he is without sin. Let that man cast the first stone."

Shocked silence. Then a slowly moving rumble of voices through the mob. But the man stayed still, hands open and outstretched. He was quickly flanked by what seemed a small and ragged guard of men. And he simply stood there. The crowd seemed confused, uncomfortable in his gentle but unwavering gaze. Slowly, they began to disperse— even the hateful priest and the Pharisees—they moved away!

He relaxed his arms, and dropped the stone in the dirt before me. Tranced by the sight, I reached out and touched it.

Held it in my hand. I turned my face up to him. He gazed at me for a long time. Looking in his face, I felt so many things—I wanted to cry—I wanted to laugh—I wanted to fall into this man's arms in gratitude and relief.

He reached down and touched my chest just over my beating heart.

It felt like it might burst for joy.

Expanding—becoming more than just myself.

Filling up with an energy, with life.

I felt safe.

I felt treasured.

When at last I could speak, I could only utter:

"Rabbi."

THE REPENTANT SINNER

Abandoned by the exiting crowd, Lazarus knelt next to me.

"Teacher. Please—you must allow us to show you gratitude and hospitality." The Teacher and his company walked with us to our house.

I walked at his side all the way.

On his other side, I saw the man who knelt to pick up the stone.

The Teacher called him Peter. This Peter did not meet my eye.

No one spoke, but I felt light. Joyful. At the house, we all washed our feet with water to cleanse them from the dust of the road and therefore cast off the day before entering. Lazarus showed the men to the table as Martha hurried into the kitchens to rouse the servants to prepare the meal.

As the Teacher sat, I felt a sudden rush of purpose— running to fetch the jar we kept near the hearth, I returned to the teacher and opened the lid. A lovely fragrance filled the room as I poured out the oil from the jar over the teacher's feet. To honor him. To single him out as most revered.

I wept in joy, wetting his feet with my tears. Discovering that in my haste, I had brought no cloth, I grabbed my long hair to wipe his feet dry.

He reached down and touched my head. Again—that feeling of expanding. Expanding beyond the confines of myself—and being allowed to do so. Becoming More. I felt dizzy.

All the company listened as the teacher told them this story.

"Once there was a rich man who lived in a grand home. At his gate lay a beggar, longing to eat what scraps fell from the rich man's table, but the rich man refused him. The beggar died at the rich man's gate and the angels carried him to Abraham's side. The rich man also died. In Hades, where he was in torment, he looked up and saw Abraham far away, with the beggar by his side. He called to him, 'Father Abraham, have pity on me—I am in agony in this fire.'

"But Abraham replied, 'In your lifetime you received your good things, while this man received bad things. Now he is comforted.'

"The rich man pleaded, 'Then I beg you, father, send this man to my family for I have five brothers. Let him warn them. If someone from the dead goes to them, they will repent.'

"Abraham said, 'If they do not listen to Moses and the Prophets, they will not be convinced even if someone rises from the dead. Blessed are those who have not seen and yet believe.'"

I sat, rapt by his words.

I wanted to know everything he knew.

I asked question after question. Some men of his company, especially the one called Peter, seemed uncomfortable with my having a conversation with the Teacher. Peter seemed to try to joke, saying, "My Lord, let the woman cease to question that we may also speak."

Martha even came in from the kitchen to scold me for not helping her with serving our guests. I was apologetic: "I am behaving badly. Please do not be angry with me. I have so many questions."

Yeshua smiled, "Question what you will. There is much you must learn, Mary."

The evening grew dark and Yeshua's company was preparing to leave when a servant rushed into Lazarus, urging him to come to the window.

In the distance, there appeared a line of dancing light, coming steadily toward the house.

Torches. The priest who had accused me at the Temple was leading a mob toward our house. Separated from Yeshua's powerful words by the soft cushion of time passing, he was bold again. Martha grabbed Lazarus and spoke close in his ear. Lazarus nodded and came to Yeshua.

"Teacher, it will be safer for you and your company to leave quickly," Martha implored. "We have many paths behind the house that lead out of our land and toward Galilee. Please—will you take our sister Mary with you? Please, teacher. She is not safe here. Keep

Mary with you for a time. Until the incident passes and the priest's outrage fades."

We could see the torches now. Setting fire to the olive trees at the front of the house.

Lazarus sent the servants to fetch water to quench the fire and prepared himself to meet the men at our doorstep. I was not afraid—but eager to go with Yeshua. This man had saved my life—of course I fell in love with him. He took my hand and turned to his followers.

"Come," he said.

We hurried out the back doors and out on to the orchard paths that I had come to know so well.

And so it was that I first led Yeshua's disciples.

Away from the house at Bethany.

Away from my old life and into the life God had planned.

A life I never could have imagined.

THE ROAD: SO LOVED

I expected that I would be secondary to the men in Yeshua's company. One of a small, faceless number of women who also came to follow him.

Anonymous.

And content to be so—content to listen to him teach in the towns and synagogues we visited. But when we would settle for another night, camping on hillsides or in open fields, he would seek me out.

Talking simply and without guise, he would ask me about myself.

I told him about my own mother and father, about my marriage and my second family at Bethany. How I loved Lazarus and Martha.

He asked me if I felt unfortunate.

Was I unhappy to have been married to a man who died so soon?

I had never thought much about that.

I said God must have wed me to him so that I would be brought together with Lazarus and Martha. That I was grateful and praised God for it.

"Why do you love them so?" He asked.

"Because they loved me, even though they didn't have to."

I told him about the trick with the bedsheets. The gardens I loved to walk. How Lazarus and I had developed our own way of talking together—our own language—and how he taught me to read and write.

Yeshua's brow lifted a bit—I was revealing dangerous secrets.

But I could not do otherwise. I knew I wanted to give him all of me.

He smiled, took my face in both his hands. He leaned in very close to my face and I felt the breath go out of me and then rush back in—as though Yeshua's breath had become my own.

"You are so loved, Mary."

The time that Yeshua and I spent together did not go unnoticed.

Once, I heard Peter say to Andrew: "Who is this woman who knows our Lord's secrets and is with him night and day? She takes opportunity from us. Let her leave us, for women are not worthy of life."

As I glanced over, Peter was looking at me and I knew he meant me to overhear his words.

The man with the stone. He still hated me.

A few weeks later, as Yeshua and I walked a little away from our sleeping friends, he presented me with a small, simply made scroll of papyrus. Rolling it open, I saw it was blank.

"You will be my witness."

I carried the scroll in a leather pouch that hung from the rope at my waist. No one seemed to notice.

Each day, at the end of evening meal, I would retire from the group. Yeshua taught me the holiness of silence. Time alone to meditate. To listen and to pray. And then, unseen by the others, to record what I had seen and heard.

FIRST JOURNEY
TO JERUSALEM

Soon, we would travel out of Galilee and to Jerusalem—to the Temple—for the Feast of Tabernacles.

That night, after we had retired, away from the others, Yeshua told me about a memory he held.

When he was younger and living in Nazareth, there came from Gamala a man named Judas. He traveled through the land preaching sedition—urging the people not to pay taxes to Rome or tithes to the Temple priests. This man preached that there was only one true Lord to whom we owe all things, all devotion, all honor.

Judas of Gamala and his many followers believed in a better world. They tried to gain enough strength to overthrow Roman rule in Galilee. Yeshua had heard him speak and was moved by his words. He saw him as a righteous man. The Romans arrested Judas and his followers. All were killed. To the last man. Judas of Gamala was crucified for sedition—he was called a traitor.

"I saw it done," Yeshua said. "The whole town was there. Watching. It was a horrible death."

I touched my fingers to his eyelids. He closed them..

"Rest," I said. The next day, Yeshua sent us into Jerusalem without him.

He did this for three days.

On the fourth day, we again left camp without him, but when we arrived in the city, he was already there—teaching in the Temple courtyards before a large group. A priest and a Pharisee were visible among the crowd.

As Yeshua spoke, we noticed movement in a small building next to us—the roof was falling in! No. No, a man was being lowered in a hammock of cloth down through the roof to the ground. A woman came to Yeshua.

"Please, Rabbi—he cannot walk."

The priest and the Pharisee followed us to stand near the lame man who lay on his back, reaching with open arms to Yeshua, who knelt and touched the man's forehead.

"Your sins are forgiven," he said.

The Pharisee stepped toward Yeshua and asked, "Are you sure you want to say this? It could be considered blasphemy."

The priest was aghast—"I thought only God can forgive sin!"

Yeshua did not look away from the man on the ground, but he said, "Which is easier? To say 'Your sins are forgiven' or to say 'Get up and walk'?"

Yeshua stood and reached his hand to the lame man.

"The Son of Man has authority to forgive sin."

The man began to sit up.

John and James helped him to stand, then moved away.

Very slowly, but steadily, the man walked to Yeshua's open arms.

The man wept and praised God. We were all ecstatic—we spoke praises and embraced each other. When I looked around, the priest and the Pharisee were gone. The people shouted praises. They followed Yeshua. They followed us.

Out of the city and to the hillside where we set our camp. To be near him. Two men came into our midst that night—one was the same Pharisee we had seen earlier—the other dressed in expensive robes. These two sat together near our fire. Yeshua seemed not to notice. When a quiet and more private moment arrived, as the people retreated to their own sleeping areas, the Pharisee approached Yeshua and spoke in low tones.

"I know you are a teacher sent from God," he said.

He seemed so earnest—in such need of good news.

"Will we see God, Rabbi?"

Yeshua touched his finger to the Pharisee's breast.

"Nicodemus."

The Pharisee's eyes were wide. He had not said his name.

"I tell you that you must be reborn if you are to be judged kindly by God." The Pharisee seemed lost.

"Reborn?" asked his richly dressed companion. "How can that be? How can a person be born twice?"

"Flesh births flesh. Spirit births spirit," Yeshua replied.

"We are not born believing—we are born in belief itself—in God's truth. It is our earthly life that takes that purity and hides it. You must find that truth again. This is what it means to be reborn.

"I come to give you that truth. God has not sent me to condemn this world. He sent me to save it."

Again, Yeshua set his finger on the Nicodemus' breast.

The Pharisee breathed in sharply and touched his hand to Yeshua's foot. Then he left us, nodding his head and murmuring to himself.

Peter hissed, "Teacher! This Pharisee reports to the Temple priests—to Caiaphas himself! The Roman soldiers will be sent to arrest us!"

"Us?"

"You," Peter simpered.

"You have nothing to fear from that man. From any man. Do what is right and serve God."

I saw the richly clothed man slip away into the darkness.

THE SERMON ON THE MOUNT

On the fifth morning, we all traveled to the Temple together.

It was tax day.

The people were tense and agitated. The rage against Rome was old and deeply rooted. Decades of taxation so heavy that people lost their homes—even their families, selling themselves as slaves to pay Caesar. No man was so hated as the tax collector—a Jew who robbed his own people in the name of Rome.

A group of men were voicing their grievances—one, a man with a deep scar running across his cheek and up into his scalp, declared, "We are barely surviving—not living as God promised! There is not enough food—our traditions of forgiving debt and offering food and hospitality are dead because we are hungry. Hunger makes bad neighbors."

The tax collectors looked nervous, sitting at their tables, accepting coins, livestock, anything the Romans would accept as payment.

The scarred man, seeing Yeshua, said, "You! They call you 'teacher' —what do you say? Are the tax collectors not traitors to Israel—to the Jews? Are they not hated by God?"

Yeshua said: "Two men went to the Temple to pray. One, a Pharisee and the other a tax collector. The Pharisee made a great show of his piety and praised God loudly saying, 'I thank you, Oh Lord, that I am not like other men. Certainly, I am a better man than this tax collector.' The tax collector would not even lift his eyes to God, but prayed, 'Lord, have mercy on me. I am a sinner.' God blessed the tax collector, but not the Pharisee. For he who exalts himself shall be humbled, and he who humbles himself shall be exalted."

Yeshua turned to one of the tables. A small, timid man sat looking down at ledgers and scales, weeping.

The man looked up only slightly and said, "Pray for me, Teacher. I am in hell."

"Levi!" cried the man next to him at the table, "Hold your tongue! You do your job because there is no choice."

Thomas turned to Peter: "No choice but to rape his own people."

Peter agreed, "There's nothing good in any of that pack of wolves." Yeshua reached out his hand and Levi, the tax collector, rose.

He walked away with us to the hillside, abandoning his table, his profession, his family and all he had known.

Levi joined our number and became Matthew. Many people had heard this exchange in the courtyard and we were again followed by a great number of them. They gathered near us, waiting for Yeshua to speak. A man mocked by the Temple priests for eating and drinking wine with sinners, mocked for his acceptance of the undesirable as his own disciples, even embracing a tax collector—they came to the hillside. The poor. The oppressed. The sight of them, and especially of their children—unfed, unprotected—pained my heart. Some of the children cried with hunger, held in the arms of mothers who looked toward us with pleading eyes. We looked out at the multitude.

"Yeshua, they are hungry."

He looked up at us—his disciples.

"Feed them," he said.

Thomas was aghast. "How can we feed them? We have almost nothing!"

"Bring me what you have," Yeshua said.

Andrew brought Yeshua a basket. It held, as Thomas had said, almost nothing. Some bread. Two little fish.

My heart felt like a stone, sitting in the pit of my stomach.

Yeshua lifted the basket high.

"Father, we thank you for what we are about to receive."

I was struck by these words and felt myself breathe in—fast and deep. Exhaling, I looked at Yeshua. Holding my gaze, he smiled wide and lowered his hands, presenting a basket overflowing with fish.

"Feed them."

What we were about to receive.

He knew it would be so! The miracle had already come into being because God the Father heard the prayer before it was uttered.

Yeshua seemed now to almost glow with joy.

He had expected the miracle. He knew.

We were all elated—offering fish and bread to every outstretched hand. Dipping into the basket again and again and never coming up empty.

The pure joy of feeding a desperately hungry person. It is so expansive—so uncontainable—we were all crying and laughing at the same time.

I looked out at the crowd, sitting and eating.

Offering food to their children with such relief and joy. I felt a gratitude deeper than I had ever known.

And there, among the people, I saw the Pharisee Nicodemus and his well-dressed friend. Eating with the people. Wiping at their own tears.

Yeshua began to speak: "Blessed are the poor in spirit, for theirs is the kingdom of heaven."

He moved through the crowd. To a widow: "Blessed are those who mourn, for they shall be comforted."

To a small boy with a shy smile: "Blessed are the meek for they will inherit the earth."

To Nicodemus—walking right up to the Pharisee: "Blessed are those who hunger and thirst for righteousness, for they shall be filled."

To Nicodemus' yet unnamed friend: "Blessed are the merciful, for they will be shown mercy."

To a little girl happily eating one of the fish: "Blessed are the pure in heart for they will see God."

Walking up to one of the Roman guards, who were now always nearby: "Blessed are the peacemakers, for they will be called children of god."

Then he came back toward us—his disciples.

He took my hand. He took John's hand:

"Blessed are those who are persecuted because of righteousness, for theirs is the kingdom of heaven. God is always with you!" Yeshua called out.

"Pray to Him and He will hear you!"

The crowd cheered and offered noisy, happy praise to God. Songs of joy.

The compelling power of this one —what hearing his words did to people—brought them together. Brought them hope. Made them feel safe. Important to someone.

Treasured.

That is truly a miracle.

The energy, the hope, the knowledge that things could change for them—within them—became real for them. They were changed through him.

They called him Messiah.

I knew without doubt that because of him—they could change the world.

We would change the world.

LET THE CHILDREN COME TO ME

Children were drawn to Yeshua.

Children see truth, though they do not understand the power of this blessing or what it means. They cannot be fooled—their purity of spirit will out a fraud. Yeshua would bend low and embrace them, looking deep into their faces, as if trying to memorize them.

Once, I asked him about the children—what was it that he saw when he looked at them that way?

He said this: "My birth into this world came at great cost."

The prophets had predicted the coming of a new king who would lead the people of Israel. A great star would appear and this descendant of the line of David would be born in Bethlehem.

When that star rose, when the kings of the east came in search of that promised ruler, Herod was afraid. So afraid of this infant and who he would become that he ordered all male babes in the land killed to protect and preserve one life—his own.

But Yeshua's parents were warned in a dream to leave that place.

Yeshua—the newborn king—lived.

I was shocked. I had heard the prophecy in my own childhood.

Everyone knew about Herod's massacre of the children.

The slaughter of the innocents was our nation's deepest grief.

"When I look at the children, I see the sacrifice of the innocent, who died so that the scriptures would be fulfilled. They are always with me."

THE WEDDING AT CANA

Yeshua received word of a wedding in his mother's family, and so we traveled to Galilee to the city of Cana to attend. It was a very modest celebration—these were not rich people—but everyone was joyful and accepting of our number in their company.

Yeshua led me to a woman sitting under the shade of a fig tree. When she saw us, she got shakily to her feet and embraced Yeshua.

The mother.

She looked frail. Often during that day, I remember, she would lean on something and breathe with her eyes closed until she could recover.

She sat next to me at table for the meal. Everyone was talking and laughing, but she seemed so alone somehow. I asked her about Yeshua.

I imagined he must have been an unusual child.

She lit up. "Oh—he was such a puzzlement!"

She smiled. With the gate now open, she walked right in and began to tell me stories of her boy. She became earnest when she told me about bringing Yeshua to the Temple in Jerusalem when he was only forty days old, to present him to God, as was tradition.

"My husband went to purchase two doves for sacrifice. While he was gone, a stranger—an old man—came to me and asked to hold Yeshua. I let him. He looked at Yeshua and began to weep.

"He told me that he knew in his soul that he would not die until he had seen the newborn king of the Jews and now he had.

"He felt it. He knew it. He offered praise to God.

"He kissed my head and asked God's blessing on me.

"Before he went his way, he seemed to be struck by something.

"He was motionless for a moment and then closed his eyes and said, 'This child will rise up and bring down many in Israel. The thoughts of many hearts will be revealed.'

"His eyes opened and he looked into my face. 'A sword must pierce your soul as well, daughter.'

"And then he was gone. My husband returned with the doves. I said nothing to him of the old man. I just wanted to leave the Temple quickly. It felt like an unsafe place for Yeshua to be. I have never known peace in that Temple."

Her tone became more hushed.

"When Yeshua was twelve years old, we went for Passover, as we did every year. The days went by. Nothing remarkable happened. I was relieved when we set out to return to Nazareth. Soon, I realized that Yeshua was not in our company—I was frantic—my husband and I went back as fast as we could to search for him. We found him in the Temple—talking with the priests and scribes.

"Engaged in a full discussion with grown men. Learned men. When I questioned him, he said he needed to be in his Father's house. He spoke like a man, not a boy."

She looked pained and bewildered.

Later, as the feast became more raucous and jubilant, the servants told the master of the house that the wine had all been drunk. Yeshua's mother, hearing this, went to him. "They are out of wine," she said, looking worried.

"Why do you tell me?" Yeshua asked.

She turned to me. "It is a bad omen."

I asked Yeshua if we might help—if had any wine in our own provisions.

He said, "Go and fill the empty jars with water and bring them to me."

Soon, servants came with many jars of water and Yeshua opened his hands, saying, "Thank you Father, for what we are about to receive."

Then he turned to the servants and told them, "Take them to the host's table and pour them out."

When they did so, the table flowed with rich, red wine.

What we were about to receive.

Grasping my hand and wringing it tight, his mother whispered to me

"I don't know what he is doing. I am terrified."

Yeshua appeared and took me from his mother's side to walk out to the far gardens. He held a cup of wine. He drank and then offered the cup to me. Bringing his mouth close to mine he said "As we drink from the same cup, so do we breathe the same breath, live the same life, become one spirit. Do not hold on to anything within you, but let it flow out.

"Empty yourself to receive me. I empty myself to receive you."

I breathed myself out. I took him in.

"Listen to me," he said. "Not separate. Divine and human. Two parts of one whole. One spirit."

Breathing with him, I felt drunk—a sensation all through my body and into my soul—a longing for him and to give myself. Two breaths becoming singular—breath that circled through both of us at once.

The inside. The outside.

I could barely stand under the dizziness of its perfection.

I never wanted it to end.

"You know me," he whispered. "Mary—you will know All.

"You will carry the All as a mother carries her unborn child.

"You must care for it in the same way."

Our company went with his mother back to Nazareth to share Sabbath. Some of Jerusalem's priests and Pharisees were again at the periphery of the group—we had become almost used to their presence. The people and clergy of Nazareth, aware of Yeshua's growing fame, asked him to read the scripture. I stayed next to his mother in the back alcoves of the room with the women. But we could hear plainly.

Yeshua read the prophet's words:

"The Spirit of The Lord is upon me. He has anointed me to preach Good News to the poor; he has sent me to heal broken hearts, to proclaim liberty to captives, give vision to the blind, to restore the crushed with forgiveness, and to proclaim the kingdom of God!"

He rolled up the scroll.

"Today this scripture is fulfilled in your ears."

Silence.

And then, a voice cried, "Messiah!"

One of the Temple priests who had traveled here in our wake screamed, "What do you think you are saying?" He bolted from the synagogue, as if he were running out of a burning building.

Yeshua's mother turned to me in tears. "What is he doing?"

I held her hand tight. "Don't be afraid."

THE ROAD: MATTHEW

We did not stay in Nazareth.

After taking his mother to her house, we shared the evening meal.

No one ate much.

It was tense and no one seemed able or willing to speak.

We made hasty goodbyes and his mother did not seem unrelieved to see us go. The company was uneasy—they had witnessed too much to absorb into their simple brains. Yeshua and I walked a little ahead of the others. "They do not understand," he said.

"Let us go from here for a while. Mary—where should we go?"

I smiled—he knew where I would go: home. To see Lazarus and Martha.

"We will go in the morning."

That night in our camp, no one seemed able to sleep.

Yeshua was trying to explain his words to Peter—he had told us that the priests and Pharisees were teaching us to follow the traditions of men, not the laws of God.

"It is not what is outside a man that makes him unclean." he said, "It is what comes out from within the man that is unclean. The things that enter our mouths—our bodies—are eliminated by the body—but the things from within the man—our words, our ideas—they come from the soul.

"Only these make us unclean."

Yeshua waited.

Nothing.

Peter looked blank.

I sighed (maybe I shouldn't have done that) and said, "It is what is in a diseased spirit that makes a diseased body."

Peter bristled.

"Why do you let this woman talk so much, rabbi? Why do you love her more than all of us?"

Yeshua replied, "Why do I not love you like her? Who do you think she is? When a blind man and one who sees are both together in darkness, they are no different from one another. When the light comes, then he who sees will see the light, and he who is blind will remain in darkness."

Silence.

"Who do you think I am?"

John answered, "Some say you are John the Baptist. Others say Elijah."

Yeshua turned to me and took my face in his hands.

"Who do you say I am?"

I had not even opened my mouth to reply when Peter blurted, "You are the Son of God."

Yeshua smiled, still looking at me. "Blessed are you."

I felt a sudden tightness in my chest and a pain behind my eyes.

I saw before me blood running like a river, drowning a hill full of crosses. Blinking, I looked over at Yeshua—he too looked stricken.

His eyes stared at nothing as he said, "The Son of Man must suffer many things and be rejected by the chief priests and elders of the law. He must be betrayed and put to death."

Then he was back.

Calm.

He stretched out to his full length next to the fire and closed his eyes.

I felt ill. There was no air. No breath. I got up and walked out toward a grove of olive trees where the breeze was sweet.

Soon, I felt an arm at my elbow.

Matthew.

"Mary. The priests and scribes—they follow us everywhere now. They question him. Goad him.

They will be making report of Yeshua's words and… deeds."

I think he was afraid to say "miracle" out loud.

Matthew continued, "Telling the Sanhedrin. Caiaphas. I think it may not be safe for us to go into Jerusalem for Passover. Should we go away from here? Could you ask him to go from here? Somewhere safe?"

His face was a mix of fear and love.

"His deeds are miracles," I told him. "The priests and Pharisees have witnessed miracles. I think there can be no safe place. I think that is as it was intended."

Suddenly, he embraced me and let loose a shattered sigh. "He delivered me out of hell. I am afraid for him."

Matthew released me and walked back to where the others dozed by the fire. Afraid for Yeshua. Not for himself.

This tax collector. He knew what it was to love people.

JAMES

It was already growing dark as we neared Bethany the next evening. Andrew was sent ahead as we set up camp for the night to allow the household to prepare for our arrival. Martha always needed enough time to fuss over the house and the meals and now there were many more of us to tend to. I smiled, thinking about Martha bustling through the rooms, sending Lazarus off on a thousand different errands.

As I washed my feet and hands in a nearby pond, James came and sat next to me, dipping his feet in the cool water. He absently scratched at his beard. It always seemed to bother him. On an impulse, I reached up and scratched his hairy face for him, like I would a shaggy animal. He laughed.

"It itches," he said, "but it is a blessing that it is so thick and long."

James was a fisherman and the beard protected his face from sun and from biting bugs. He showed me a small piece of fish net that he kept with him to remind him of the wife and child he had left behind.

"To bring about the new kingdom for them," he said.

"Mary, I feel so weak because I miss them. Shouldn't my being witness to these words, these miracles, be all that I can see or feel or hear?"

James worried at the frayed piece of net between his fingers.

"If I am weak. If I am a disappointment, maybe he will not bless them. Because of me."

So much pain in his grey eyes.

"You delight his heart, James—and so, the heart of the Father. They are one and the same. Know this truth: We are all—all of us—blessed."

I took James' hands in mine and kissed them. I held my face close to his. "Blessed are those in sorrow, for they will be comforted."

James drew in a sharp breath.

I watched his eyes clear of their sad confusion.

LAZARUS

In the morning, we readied to make the short trip into Bethany.

My heart was light. The day was mild and we were all enjoying the walk toward what we knew was a friendly place. John was even humming quietly as we moved. After a time, we saw Andrew coming back to us.

He was running. He came to me right away and fell to his knees, panting. He held my ankles as he said, "Mary. Mary your brother is dead. Lazarus is dead."

I heard his words as if I were under water. They made no sense.

"No, Andrew. You are mistaken."

Breaking free from his hands, I kept walking.

"Mary! He is dead! Four days now. He is already laid in the tomb."

I kept walking, Yeshua by my side, reaching for my hand.

We kept walking.

Suddenly, Martha was in front of us: "Rabbi! I prayed for you to come!

I told Lazarus if we prayed that you would come and he would be restored. But—he died."

She looked so lost. So utterly consumed with grief. Uncomprehending. "Mary. He died."

Yeshua told her to take us to him.

At the tomb, Yeshua called for the cave to be opened.

"Teacher"—it was Thomas—"he has been four days in the tomb. It will be too horrible for Martha. For Mary."

Yeshua said nothing, pointing to the stone at the cave's mouth. After the stone was moved away, he walked in and I followed. The air already stinking of decay. Yeshua and I went next to the body and together unwrapped the face from its linen. Beautiful Lazarus. His face grey and purple. Sunken. No trace of my brother left there. My heart wrenched—I reeled in to Yeshua's arms. Too stricken to form words. I could only look at him, bringing my face to his. Breathe...

Inside. Outside.

I felt it in my head, my chest, my heart.

Yeshua whispered, "Father, I thank you that you have heard me."

He turned and breathed in to Lazarus' empty face. "Wake up, Lazarus. Come forth."

When we heard Martha's strangled gasp, we looked over at our brother. The linens around his body began to quiver, then shake violently. A sound—

unearthly—a cat's mewl—a baby's cry—a soul in darkness. It cut into my chest like knives.

John and Luke ripped the linens away from the body, retching as they did.

Slowly, Lazarus sat up.

He grabbed John and Luke with each hand.

"Light," he gasped out, "Bring light."

A torch appeared in the cave. It was day and the tomb was not very dark, but Lazarus' eyes had no light in them. They were black. The torch swam before his pale face. He shook his head and I watched the black in his eyes recede to small pinpoints within their familiar amber irises.

He looked at me—"I do not know why I am here."

Yeshua took Lazarus' face in his hands. "Your sisters' strong love and faith, they have spoken to bring you back together with them. They believed it possible through me."

We helped Lazarus to his feet and toward the mouth of the cave.

To the crowd that had gathered, Yeshua said, "See! The love and faith shown to me by Martha and Mary have saved their brother. How many more of you can be saved by such faith? Such love? Lazarus is raised from ultimate darkness. I am the resurrection, and the life: he that believes in me, though he were dead, yet shall he live: Believe this. For you will witness it all again—soon."

Lazarus was helped toward the house—he was not steady on his feet—and the crowd was praising God and calling "Messiah!" and kneeling in our wake.

I looked back. There he was. That same man who had been with Nicodemus. In different robes now.

Sanhedrin.

He fought with himself not to kneel in the dirt, eyes filled with tears.

I asked Yeshua, "Is he the one who will give you over to our enemies?"

Yeshua answered, "No. That place belongs to one much closer."

As I glanced back at our company, Peter looked away and went inside.

We stayed at the house several days. Yeshua was exhausted.

I spent treasured time with my Martha.

We tended to our brother.

Lazarus stayed in the shadows inside the house with his servant, Micah. Lazarus was never to be alone. He would become frightened and cry out. One lovely morning, Martha and I walked out into the orchards that belonged to the household. We shared memories of our years together. After the death of my in-laws, she became wholly devoted to Lazarus.

She never married.

Lazarus never married.

Unheard of—there were no bachelors in Israel. In fact, I did not know there was a word for "bachelor" until I came to this place. None of my brothers were "bachelors." They were more widowers—having left their families to become disciples. In our company, only the Teacher had a companion. Lazarus was always a bit suspect to the townspeople. More whispers and assumptions. It was agonizing for Lazarus, but he knew it better to be whispered about than publicly condemned for something he would never bring himself to be.

You see, my brother Lazarus was in love. With Micah.

Martha and I discussed how best to address the situation.

Should Micah be sent away? I told her No. Love is of God.

Martha wasn't listening. She was gazing at the horizon cresting over the hills.

She said to me, "You should stay here. With us. Too many people know who you are. The priests. The Pharisees. They will not let you alone much longer, you know. They will have you all killed. Stay here. This is your home. We love you. We need you more than he does. He has many followers."

I looked at her girlish face.

"Martha, do not look to keep me here. My place is with him. I know the storm is coming. I can feel it— the very air is changing. Buzzing all around us. Something is coming, Martha and you must believe with all your heart. With all the strength of the love you have held for me. Believe. For Lazarus.

"Believe that God has raised him from ultimate darkness.

"Believe. For Martha.

"Believe that God is with you."

In that moment, Martha looked so very young.

"The prophecies," I told her. "They are coming to be."

She fell into my arms and I held her with all my strength.

"He is the Son of God, isn't he, Mary?"

I have never wept such joyful tears.

Returning to the house, I saw the Sanhedrin who had accompanied Nicodemus. I had had enough. If this man was a threat, I wanted to know who he was.

"Sir", I said, walking up to face him. "What would you have here?"

He looked down at his feet.

"I mean no harm—would you, please, ask... him. To pray for me?"

I was surprised. "Ask him yourself."

He gently shook his head. "It is enough that you bring him my words. He who was promised is come. Forgive me my sins."

He was sincere!

"What is your name?" I asked.

He looked up a bit. "I am Joseph. Born in Arimathea."

"Blessed are those who hunger and thirst for righteousness, Joseph, for they will be filled."

He was smiling now and said, "Rejoice, Oh daughter of Zion—see your king comes to you, righteous and bringing salvation, gentle and riding on a donkey. He will proclaim peace to all nations and his rule will extend to the ends of the Earth."

I recognized the words of the prophet.

"Joseph. Go home to Jerusalem and make ready for Passover. Go prepare the way of the Lord."

I arrived at the house in time to see Yeshua sending John and James out toward the city and I knew. I looked at him and I knew.

"They are fetching you a donkey."

THE ANNOINTED ONE

We gathered for the evening meal. I washed Yeshua's feet with water, then again brought the jar from the hearthside and poured out its fragrant balm over his feet, rubbing them with my hands. I rose and poured out all the remaining balm over his head, caressing my hands over his face, his throat, his shoulders. Peter balked uneasily.

He hated to see Yeshua and I touch like this.

Judas said, "Such a waste—that oil could have been sold for a good price and the money used to feed the poor. To do good works."

Yeshua flared—just for a moment: "Why do you trouble her? You will always have the poor with you, but you will not always have me." He took my hands and brought them to his face.

"She anoints my body to prepare for my funeral. Wherever the gospel is proclaimed, what she has done will be told in praise of her. She will be called Magdalene. The woman who knows all. She is my tower, the strength that will sustain you when I am gone."

I washed Lazarus' feet with water, then each of the company.

Coming at last to Peter. I looked up into his face.

"Peace be with you, Peter." We must not be enemies.

Later that night, Yeshua and I were alone. He was lying on the bed, watching me as I sat with a candle, recording the day's events in the scroll. Suddenly, he sighed aloud and looked stricken with grief.

He held out his arms. I folded myself in his embrace.

"They still don't understand, do they?"

HUMBLE, AND RIDING ON A DONKEY

We set out for Jerusalem and the Passover feast. As we reached the edge of Bethany, John and James waited for us with a man who held the bridle of a small donkey. The man knelt before Yeshua.

"I am blessed to offer you this animal. You are he who has been promised to come."

Yeshua knelt and took the man's face in his hands. "You shall see my kingdom."

The man almost seemed to faint with joy.

I removed my outer cloak and lay it across the donkey's back. The animal was nervous at all the fuss being made over him, as if he knew that it was a precious burden he was about to bear. I liked its face—it had a beard that made me think of James. I scratched its beard and cooed a bit and it calmed as Yeshua sat upon its back. As we neared Jerusalem, our number steadily increased. Pilgrims appeared on all sides, laying palm fronds on the ground for the donkey to walk on—singing praise.

Yeshua was famous.

PROPHECY

Yeshua came down from the little donkey's back and walked toward the Temple courtyards.

Arriving at the Temple, Yeshua was calm. He did not speak or try to teach, he looked like just another pilgrim, come to observe Passover. Priests, scribes and Roman guards. They seemed to be in every corner. Watching. We gave them nothing to see. Nothing to report to Caiaphas or to the Roman governor, Pilate.

Yeshua and I separated—he going to the inner part of the Temple and I remaining with the women. There, I was approached by an ancient, white haired waif called Anna.

"I remember him," she said.

"I saw him—here at Temple—he was a baby and his parents presented him to God with a sacrifice of doves. He is the one whose coming was foretold. Herod could not destroy him. And you—you will witness. Never turn your eyes away for a second—no matter how painful. You must see the All."

She was gripping my hand tight in her bony fingers.

"Mother, I will," I said.

That night, camped on the hill outside the city, I told Yeshua of the old woman's words to me.

"The All," he said. "We are two whole beings and yet each of us is half of one great truth. Two that make one and as one, both continue. This is what God made you to be."

He looked over at the shadowy figures of our sleeping company.

"You will lead them when I am gone. Give them this knowledge."

We slept. I had no dreams.

TURNING THE TABLES

In the morning, Yeshua was restless, as if the night's sleep had not restored him. When I asked he said that he had been troubled by dreams.

Our preparations were hasty and we hurried down the hill toward the city. Once in the Temple courtyard, Yeshua's agitation began to pique.

"The slums of Jerusalem overflow! Families are lost because they cannot repay what they have borrowed to make sacrifice in the Temple. Money they have borrowed from vipers in the same Temple. This is not love of God, it is an affront to God!"

Seeing again the seated money changers, Yeshua suddenly took Judas by the hand and walked directly to them, upending the tables and sending coins flying everywhere. Holding Judas' hand, he said to the crowd, "Be wary, for the coins of this Temple can only purchase the destruction of your soul!"

Yeshua released the caged doves, turning on those who were there to buy and to sell animals for sacrifice in the Temple.

"You make my house a den of thieves!" he cried.

Surprised money lenders scattered. The people were transfixed. So oppressed for so long, a strangled cry of hope became a roar of elation.

We began to hear "Hosanna!"

It seemed as if the children appeared from nowhere. "Hosanna the Son of David!" they sang.

Yeshua bent low and held out his arms to them, searching their faces as if he saw in them all the babes who were slaughtered by Herod.

Sacrificed for his sake.

I looked around—Roman guards. Pharisees. Nicodemus.

Nicodemus stepped forward and asked, "Teacher— is it wrong for us to pay taxes to Rome?"

Was he asking Yeshua to reject Rome? To incite the people?

The man I had seen before—the one with the horrible scar on his face—was there. He seemed on fire with the question.

"No taxes for Rome!" he cried. "No taxes for Rome!"

His companion grabbed his arm. "Barabbas! Be quiet! You will get us all arrested!"

The man Barabbas called out to Yeshua and ran toward him.

"They used our Temple money to build an aqueduct! Our tithes to the Temple—stolen from us—and when we protested, we were slaughtered like dogs in the streets! If you have come to be our king, deliver us from Roman oppression! As Moses delivered us from slavery in the deserts of Egypt! Tell us—shall we pay taxes to Rome?"

Yeshua reached down and picked up a coin from the dirt.

"Whose face is on this coin?"

Barabbas answered, "Caesar's!" and he spat on the ground.

"Then render unto Caesar that which is Caesar's," Yeshua began. "But render unto God that which is God's."

Cheers of praise from the people.

Yeshua went to Barabbas and gently touched his chest.

Barabbas fell backward as if struck.

"Do you understand, Barabbas?"

The scarred face seemed to transform—he was silent. His friend grabbed him up and pulled at him, moving him away from the courtyard.

Joseph of Arimathea—the Sanhedrin—came closer. He was earnest.

He asked, "Rabbi—which commandment is the greatest?"

The crowd was rapt.

The Sanhedrin asking humbly for answers! From Yeshua!

"Love the Lord your God with all your heart, all your mind and all your soul. This is the first. The second—love your neighbor as you love yourself. All the laws and the prophets hang on these. Nothing else matters. Every obscene detail of life within these walls—the practices of unclean souls—they offend the Father."

He saw a child before him, staring up at his face. He bent down to him, smiling, calmly telling him, "Do you see this great building we are in? Every stone of this Temple will be brought down. Not one stone will be left standing."

The child gaped and then laughed. Yeshua stood.

"Destroy this temple and I will raise it up in three days. Do not fix your salvation on these rocks."

The crowd exploded. Shouting praise and calling for blessings on Israel.

Looking around, I saw Roman guards, moving priests away from the courtyard, shaking their heads as if denying them the chance to engage with the commotion. Yeshua caught the Sanhedrin Joseph, by the arm and led him away from the noise. They spoke briefly and Joseph left the Temple. Returning to my side, he said to the company;

"Come. I have arranged for the evening meal."

We walked out of the Temple grounds, trailed by jubilant pilgrims, songs of the children in our ears.

Judas was not with us.

THE SUPPER IN THE UPPER CHAMBER

Joseph the Sanhedrin led us to the upper chamber of a building he owned away from the center of town. While he laid out a supper—according to Yeshua's wishes—I retired to an unseen, silent corner to write what had happened.

"Not one stone of this Temple will be left standing. All things of the physical world will erode and pass away. It is not the earthly Temple—the stones—that are our salvation, it is the temple of self—the soul in complete experience with God. The particles within and without us that make up everything. Can it be?

"Are we so close to God and do not know it?"

These would be the last words I wrote for a very long time.

Judas was in the room when I returned. Joseph did not ask to join us, but said he would be close by should we have need for anything.

Yeshua handed me a basin of water and we went together around the table, washing the feet of our company. Afterward, we sat together. I was at his right side, Peter at his left. Yeshua told us we were celebrating the Passover meal one day early. Judas looked taken aback—this was a violation of Jewish tradition. We all knew this, but no one protested.

If Yeshua called for this, this was how it must be. We were all quiet.

There was a tension in the air—waiting for Yeshua to speak.

The only sounds were tearing of bread. Pouring out of wine.

Suddenly, Yeshua grasped my hand. He became rigid and I felt my own body become tense and immobile. My eyes closed.

I breathed in sharply, exhaling into this vision:

I saw a man before me.

The high priest, Caiaphas.

"My son, the true Messiah will unite the people of Israel, not divide them. Bring Yeshua to me so that we may talk discreetly. Help me prevent a terrible disaster, Judas."

As my breath returned, I opened my eyes and looked to Yeshua.

He held my hand tightly and said nothing.

Not him.

He loved Yeshua—hung on his every word—ate them like nourishment. Devoted. I looked at Judas' kindly face.

No.

Not him.

Yeshua said, "This is our last meal together. One of you here will betray me."

They all looked around the table at each other.

"The Son of Man will go, for it is written."

Was that my voice that spoke?

There was no more eating or drinking at the table.

We sat in silence, Yeshua's hand in mine. After a time, Peter stood, saying he would pour more wine. The others shifted about. Judas passed near. Yeshua took his arm.

"Go quickly and do it."

Yeshua let time pass, assuring that Judas would reach his destination.

Then he said—

"Come, the hour is late and I want to pray."

THE PASSION IN THE GARDEN

At the foot of the hill at Gethsemane there stood a small olive grove. Untended. Abandoned. Its Jewish owners taxed into ruin, perhaps even slavery, by the Roman empire. Not a likely bridal chamber.

Yeshua turned to us. "Stay here and wait. Be watchful."

Offering his hand to me, he said, "Come with me. I must pray with all my self."

Under a pale moon, Yeshua caressed my face.

"Beloved, I am making you a widow again."

I wept. How would I pray for the strength to let my world end?

He said "Magdalene—listen to me. Do not listen to your fear—listen to me.

"Blessed one, in you I will perfect all mysteries.

"You are the All, Magdalene. You will lead them.

"They are your children now. Your apostles.

"Teach them. All that you have experienced—they will experience through you and come to the truth: The kingdom of God is always with you. It lives within. It is the perfect marriage of the divine and the human —there is no separation of God from man. Love cannot be separated from love. Nor truth from truth. Teach them.

"All that you have witnessed through me will be possible to you, too.

"You will carry the true gospel—the true kingdom— out into the world."

Startled by a noise, we went to find the others.

They all lay sleeping under the darkness of the trees.

The sound we heard was James, crying in his sleep.

Yeshua's voice was like that of an anguished child. "Could none of you stay awake?"

Roused, they all sat up.

"I still have much to do—can you not stay vigilant with me?"

"Master—I will not fall away." It was Peter.

Suddenly, I saw a vision of Peter—walking through a river of blood. Walking away from where Yeshua lay broken in red water, stepping over my own drowning body as he went.

Then I was back in the garden again.

Yeshua seemed about to explode in anguish. He grabbed Peter's shoulders, and weeping, he leaned in close to Peter's ear: "I tell you. Before the sun rises you will deny me three times."

He released Peter and sank to his knees, stricken.

Peter was about to speak and I held my fingers to his lips and shook my head. Touching him, I saw for an instant a memory of pain. A beautiful little boy with long, dark curls, crying. I felt sorrow—shunned by children at play. Abandoned.

I slid my fingers from his mouth to hold his chin in my hand. I wanted in that moment to hold him close. Take the pain from him. The fear in Peter's eyes softened. Yeshua, seeing this, seemed to be almost restored.

He took my arm.

"Come with me."

Standing in the dark, empty garden. Bridal chamber. Yeshua and I, facing each other. So close. "Look at me," he said. "Let go of what you think you know. Look at me and see past body, past face, past eyes. Look.

"See the infinite and enter.

"You know me. My blessed one, you will tower over all my disciples. They will receive the mysteries from you."

I saw—past the body, past the earth we stood on. I felt all the particles of myself releasing from the others, dissolving into air—becoming spirit—I felt these particles melt into that infinite as I entered into it-absorbed by it—peace and light and infinite perfection. Complete union. I could feel it, though I had no body. I could see it, though I had no eyes. And then, though I had no ears, I heard it.

Whispered, but sounding within and without, throughout all eternity:

"This is my kingdom."

I would show them.

Falling back to earth. Jolted awake by an invisible blow. I was looking in Yeshua's eyes again. Breathing in and out together. Infinite. One.

"Rabbi."

Not my voice.

We looked over, past our sleeping companions.

Judas.

And behind him.

Torches.

Coming toward us like the slow moving line of a fire as it eats an orchard.

AN EYE FOR AN EYE

We followed the soldiers to the home of the high priest, Caiaphas.

As we neared the gates of the house, I stepped away to wait, knowing I would not be allowed inside. I looked around me.

None of my brothers were anywhere in sight—only two guards, left here to watch the gate. I was looking at them both when suddenly, I could no longer see them, or the gate.

I saw a dark hallway. Candles lit along the wall. I was moving forward, propelled by the unseen arms. Before me, I saw different men—robed in the garments of the Temple.

And ahead of them, in front of my eyes, another man. Exquisitely robed. Small. Grey. Caiaphas.

He was looking right at me.

"Yeshua of Nazareth" he said.

In his eyes I saw remnants of fear. I felt his thoughts race in his mind—remembering the riots over the aqueduct. Roman soldiers disguised as Jews. Pulling swords not from their uniforms, but from under Jewish robes. Remembering the blood. The screams.

Caiaphas was seeing his own memory—a slaughter of innocents as cruel as Herod's had been.

I knew his thoughts. He was terrified.

This teacher before him had gained too large, too strong a following—what if they disrupted the Temple? Denounced taxation? Who could say what Pilate would do? He had already threatened to close the Temple at the first sign of trouble—Passover would be lost. The holiest of days would be lost to his people. Everything would be lost. This troublesome prophet must be dealt with before the feast day.

"Are you the son of God?" Caiaphas' voice quaked as he spoke.

So much fear. That Yeshua could cause the end of all he knew.

Caiaphas lived under Rome's thumb, but he lived very well.

Wiping the slate clean to start new was not to be imagined.

Again: "Are you the son of God?"

I felt Yeshua's voice in my throat.

"Yes. It is you who say it. You will see the Son of Man seated at the right hand of God and coming on the clouds of heaven."

"Blasphemer!" Caiaphas cried. "You have heard it! Blasphemy!"

Tearing his fine robes, he ordered the guards who held Yeshua's arms, "Take him! Send word to Pilate that we are coming to his quarters. Now!"

As my vision began to fade, I caught sight of Nicodemus. Weeping silently.

Then my sight went black and I felt myself falling.

I was roused by the sound of voices: "You! You were with the Nazarene—you are one of his company!"

Blinking my eyes at the darkness, I saw the guard who had spoken—and also the one he had spoken to: Peter. "No. I do not know him."

The other guard: "I have seen you with him. You are one of his followers."

"He is nothing to do with me," Peter replied.

The two stepped closer. Peter said, "I tell you I do not know him!"

As he turned to flee, he tripped over my fallen body and tumbled to the dirt. He looked into my face and burst into bitter tears, collapsing in my arms. He was in such agony of spirit, but there was so little time.

"Find the others," I said. "Go back to the upper chamber. I will come to you there" Peter scrambled to his feet and ran from the gate. I felt very faint.

I crawled away a bit into shadow and closed my eyes.

Again, voices: "According to our law, the penalty for blasphemy is death, prefect." Caiaphas.

"Then execute him." A new voice. Deep. Annoyed.

I opened my eyes.

Pilate.

"Prefect, the Sanhedrin is forbidden to do so. We need your help. He has incited much unrest, and unrest—sedition—is contagious. He calls himself our king. A capital crime against Rome."

Pilate turned to look into Yeshua's face. My face.

"Are you the king of the Jews?"

A smile played at the corners of Pilate's mouth.

We spoke: "My kingdom is not of this world."

Pilate was still smiling "But you are a king?"

"You are right to call me a king. I have come into the world to testify to the truth."

The smile gone, Pilate seemed almost entranced. Walking away from where Caiaphas stood, Pilate came close to us, his eyes alert: "What is the truth?"

He seemed in earnest. I could not speak, but only see the weary, disappointed man Pilate had become. Receiving no reply, he sighed and said, "This man is guilty of nothing more than delusion."

Caiaphas appeared at the prefect's side.

"If he is released, his followers will riot in the streets. Surely the emperor would not be pleased. He would send in his army."

Pilate turned on Caiaphas and hissed: "Threatening me with my own emperor is unwise, priest."

Pilate was silent a moment. Then, that small smile returned.

"I have a man in my cells awaiting crucifixion for his crimes. I will employ the Passover amnesty—let your Jews decide who will be set free: this murderer or your prophet. Guard—take this king to the stock."

Pilate walked away and Caiaphas stood, looking into our face. As the guards began to move Yeshua, I could feel myself separate from him and return to my other self—standing again before Pilate's gate.

I gathered myself up and ran for the others in the upper chamber.

I told them to follow me.

FLESH AND FLESH

As we reached the court, I saw that even at this hour, a crowd had gathered outside Pilate's praetorium. My brothers and I could not enter the inner courtyard—it was too full of people. I pushed my way to the front of the crowd and up against the bars of the gate itself.

Yeshua.

Stripped and on his knees, his shackled wrists tied to the scourging post. The lash, high in the air and then—down.

I screamed—pain seared through me.

I grabbed at the body beside me—John.

"Sister?"

I could not breathe. Each stroke that came down in the courtyard sliced across my back—racked my spine.

Again. Again. As though it was never going to stop. Suddenly—nothing. Searing heat across my body.

Blood in my eyes.

I fell sweating into the dust at the gate. John came to help me.

He touched my back and I screamed.

When he took his hand away it was wet with blood.

In the courtyard, the guards had brought Yeshua a crown made from the branches of a thorn bush. They pushed it down on his scalp.

Fire!

I reached up to wipe my brow—my fingers sticky and red.

The torture over, Yeshua collapsed and vomited.

I tasted blood in my mouth.

The soldiers were dragging him from the stock and John quickly carried me away in his arms before my state could be clearly noticed.

WHAT SHALL I DO WITH HIM, THEN?

In a dark place, hands on me—washing my body with water that burned like acid. Water offered to my mouth. A bit of bread soaked in wine.

A voice: "Mary."

Opening my swollen eyes, I saw a woman I knew.

The mother.

Come to Jerusalem to celebrate the Passover feast and instead shown the mouth of hell.

A knock. Two men entered. Voices.

John: "We must return to the courtyard—the decision is to be made soon. Sister, stay here with this good man."

I turned my eyes to the man.

The Sanhedrin—Joseph of Arimathea.

I refused. "Look at me—at my body—I am already there with him.

Take my body to the place where I am."

At the gate, I looked about. No familiar face inside the courtyard—many were well dressed, clean. None of our company here outside the gate, save John, who supported my body—and the mother. How old she looked, amid the deafening crowd. I reached for her, but she did not see me. Transfixed.

Staring ahead. At the bloodied, broken man that had been her boy. A horn sounded and the crowd quieted.

Pilate spoke: "Two men stand here for judgment. This man—a rebel. A thief and an instigator. A murderer. Called Barabbas."

Barabbas! Lifting my head, I strained to see the man with the angry scar running up his face. He was quiet now.

"Or—this man—who calls himself the king of the Jews."

The crowd rumbled without much conviction as though considering.

Caiaphas' voice yelling: "We have no king but Caesar!"

Like the stones of the Temple, the high priest was lost.

Looking up at his sweaty, distorted face, I felt Caiaphas' soul crack in two.

A new voice: "Release Barabbas!"

And again: "Release Barabbas!"

Another voice and another.

"It is not a fair vote," John was saying. "Look!"

The crowd inside thc gates was placed there by Caiaphas to be heard above Yeshua's followers, who remained locked outside the walls.

Pilate said to them, "What shall I do then with Yeshua, who is called the Christ? Let him be crucified? What evil has he done?"

The crowd of imposters cried out loudly: "Crucify him!"

Barabbas' eyes were wide. Recognizing Yeshua, he shook his head.

In disbelief? Or in protest of the verdict?

John said, "They will have Yeshua—Pilate cannot spare him—they will riot."

Pilate called for a basin. Washing his hands in the water, he told the mob, "I am not guilty of this man's blood. Let it be on your heads."

It would be so—the blood of the Christ on their heads and their children's.

JOURNEY OF A THOUSAND STEPS

It was full daylight now. Hot. And the son of God began the slow journey toward the end with a cross beam plank of wood upon his shoulders. Yeshua could barely move—so battered, so thirsty, so weakened. The death squad ordered a man in the crowd to help him carry his burden.

I walked, supported by John and Joseph. The mother was there.

No words spoken.

Cries in the crowd—some derisive, some anguished sobs of the believers.

I tried to look at faces—none familiar—but one. Behind all the others, one that I knew. Haunted. Eyes staring out of his scarred face.

On a hill outside the city, Yeshua lay his burden on the ground.

His helpmate was pushed aside and Joseph caught him.

"Who are you?"

The man told him, "Simon."

Joseph took both his hands and put them in mine.

I tried to speak. A crack of sound—shattering pain in my wrist.

I looked down at my hands, resting in Simon's. Distorting. Bones moving.

No blood. No wound. Only disfiguring pain. I sat sharply on the ground.

My other wrist exploding now.

"Joseph," I hissed, "take them further off!"

I could not stand for the shock of pain in my feet.

Joseph guided the mother and Simon away from where I sat in the dirt, making no sound while my body pulled itself apart.

"Eloi, Eloi lama sabachthani!"

The death squad, their work done, moved over a bit to the shade of an awaiting tent to bide their time until the three men crucified that day were dead. I crawled slowly to the foot of the cross. So close to the wood that when I looked up, Yeshua's blood dripped down on to my face.

"I thirst."

One of the soldiers soaked a sponge in wine and lifted it up to Yeshua's mouth. I felt the sour, watery liquid on my tongue and down my throat.

Yeshua lifted his head a bit: "It is finished."

He seemed to be looking out at—what? I turned my head. I saw John, Joseph, the mother, Simon. And behind them—a multitude of souls—not of this world, but the souls of Yeshua's disciples yet to come.

Kings. Holy men and women—stretching past the horizon to eternity.

"Father, into your hands, I commend my spirit."

Memories of fear. Remnants of pain. Physical pain worse than can be imagined and then so quickly forgotten—like childbirth. I imagine if you were to try to re-live it, re-feel it, you would not be able to do it.

Which is fortunate or there would be very few children born.

Pain of the body is like that.

Pain of the heart—pain of the spirit—can always be recalled.

That pain can be re-lived as sharply as the moment it was first felt.

It is one of the cruelest of mysteries.

Even now, across this sea of time, here at the end of all time, I am able to feel my heart break, remembering the depth of loss, of love, of sorrow that I felt then.

On that day.

In that moment.

In that instant when I felt the life, the breath, leave him.

Everything changed in that moment. He was so clearly no longer there.

He turned ashen and dark, limp and yet stiffly contorted all at once.

I felt, in that instant, the purest pain I have ever known.

I howled that pain—that loss—so much more violent and profound than the pain in my twisted bones. I felt I would dissolve into the sand and blow away in that final breath as he released it. I did not.

Why?

Why didn't the world simply end in that moment?

Suffocating and distorted—like being caught under a wave that keeps breaking, not letting me surface. Washing pain over me again and again. This hell continued.

Joseph had men come and cut him down from the cross. He assured me he had made all preparations—to come with him. I raised my head to see John and Simon leading the mother away. I never saw her again.

Numb now, I was carried to the outskirts just beyond the mount of crosses to an open tomb cut into the rocky hill. Here, Joseph's men laid Yeshua's body down. They brought a basin of water and sponges and bowed their heads as I washed the blood from Yeshua's skin. Offering me a length of clean linen, Joseph guided my shattered hands and set them to folding and winding the cloth around his feet, his legs, his chest, and finally his head. Covering his face. We prayed.

"We can do no more now." Joseph told me. "After the Sabbath has passed, we will attend him as it should be done."

As we stood and watched Joseph's men roll the stone over the entrance of the cave. I felt my sight begin to dim and then leave me all together. Blind.

I opened my mouth to ask for help—

Mute.

Hands on me to lift me up and carry me away, but no sound.

Deaf.

I realized after a time that I must be in the upper chamber again.

I knew someone was there with me—offering bits of food or drink to my mouth. I felt the room pressing in on me. Like being under water.

My head hurt. My chest hurt. Where was the air?

A drowsy desperation descended on me. I must have slept.

AND ON THE THIRD DAY

I awoke to a sound in the night. I opened my eyes into darkness, but I could hear... something.

Slowly, my eyes came into focus—the room was dim, but I did see the room. My brothers, asleep. The door of the chamber opened and I saw light—I saw—not the door—a great stone was rolling away from in front of the chamber.

Open—it is open.

Frantic, I searched for a vessel I had brought into the chamber—a small alabaster jar like the one we kept on the hearth in Bethany—and with it, I slipped silently from the room, descending the stairs to the street.

Staying out of sight in the pre-dawn darkness, I moved as quickly as my broken body would allow. Back over the hill of silhouetted crosses, toward the tomb. I passed a man, his robe reflecting the moon's light, kneeling in what seemed to be prayer. He did not seem to notice me and I kept moving, holding the jar tight to my chest. As I approached the place where the tomb should be, I saw the stone that Joseph's men had rolled in front of its mouth had been moved—cracked in two and lying away from the entrance of the cave.

It was open.

Thieves!

If they had seen Joseph, they must have thought this the tomb of a wealthy man and broke the stone to raid the tomb. To steal the riches of a man who had none. The profanity was too much for my exhausted heart to absorb—the jar slipped from my hands and fell to the rocky ground, opening and weeping its contents over my feet. I sank to my knees, trying to catch the escaping oils with my hands. It soaked into my robes and covered my skin in fragrant mud. In my grief, I smeared the oily mud over my face and into my hair. I lay on the ground in that same precious slop and rolled about in my agony. Finally exhausting myself, I drifted into a swooning sleep. Perhaps minutes passed. Perhaps years.

I finally stirred and felt an exquisitely sharp pain in my head. My stomach turned over and I vomited into the anointed dirt. Sobbing and crawling to the mouth of the cave, the breaking dawn revealed the shroud of linens, empty and crumpled on the ground. As I reached for it, I heard a voice behind me: "Woman—why do you weep?"

I turned my head quickly, sending a sharp and nauseating pain through my skull. It was the man I had seen earlier, kneeling in prayer. I told him, "They have taken my Lord. I do not know where he is."

His voice.

"Mary."

Not dead.

"Rabboni."

Not dead.

I lurched toward him, but he stopped me.

"Do not embrace me—I am not yet ascended to the Father.

"I balance between the realms. Go tell the others what you have seen.

"Tell them I am here."

THE UPPER ROOM

Back to the upper chamber. Back to my brothers. They would not believe what I was telling them.

"Come! Peter—John—come and see for yourselves!"

We bolted from the room, John half carrying me. At the tomb, Peter picked up the linen and looked around at the mud and oil and the forgotten jar. John was beside himself with joy—"It is the truth! He is here!"

He saw me, struggling to stand upright.

"Sister—are you well?"

"We must return to the others," I told him. "Yeshua is coming."

Back in the chamber, John told them what they had seen.

Thomas: "I will not believe it until I see him with my eyes."

I grabbed Thomas' hands—"I tell you the truth—he is risen."

He looked weary. "We are all exhausted. Sister, go lie down."

As I held tight to Thomas' hands, I felt my lungs fill with air—my chest open up with light.

I saw Thomas' eyes grow wide and heard Yeshua's voice:

"Thomas, do not doubt. I am with you. Believe because you see.

"Blessed are those who have not seen and yet, believe.

"Look. This is Mary, my beloved. My tower. The woman who knows All.

"She will proclaim to you what is yet hidden. Listen to her."

And he was gone.

Finally exhaling, my head throbbed. Thomas stared.

Others wept or laughed—almost hysterical with joy—surrounding me, kissing my hands. Peter sat very still.

"Mary," Andrew said, "what do we do now?"

Peter looked over at me:

"Yes, Mary. What do we do now?"

"We remember him."

We prepared the table. Broke bread. Shared a cup of wine.

ALONE. NOT ALONE.

When I was first without him—after the cross, after
the tomb, after his return—I could see him before
me always. Vivid. Palpable. But as the days doubled
and tripled, I was no longer able to feel that I could
reach out and touch him. It made the days hiding in
the upper chamber long and lonely. My feet felt
heavier. It was hard to command them to walk.

I was sad and confused—how could the Son of Man
become a memory?

I felt like an unfaithful wife.

How could my faith—my knowledge of him—be so
weak as to allow him to fade from my Self? Were we
not truly one being?

Joined together and with God as part of all things?

I had lost my young husband—why wasn't this
different somehow?

It made writing in the scroll impossible. It made me
anxious.

It made me careless.

In my need to stay connected to Yeshua, I shared
too much of myself—my thoughts—with the others.
Soon, I heard Peter accusing me of weakness of

faith. Saying that I could not be looked to as a teacher. A leader.

It was like slapping a sleeping child awake.

I left my self-pity and stopped remembering Yeshua as in a childish crush. We were not sweethearts.

We were partners—that partnership a living and blessed entity.

He would be as present as I allowed myself to be present. Two as one.

I took my place at the table with my brothers at what would be Yeshua's right hand. Peter looked over. I met his eye. We were motionless for a moment—only a moment—and I gestured him to sit at my right, never losing his gaze. He did so and we broke the bread and shared the wine.

Philip seemed energized this evening. "Soon we will go forth from this place to spread Yeshua's gospel. Mary—teach us what Yeshua told to you so that we can be prepared."

Peter stood. "We will rest tonight. Sleep. Tomorrow must be a day for action. We know we are not safe here. We should go out of Jerusalem to prepare"— he looked at me—"to learn from our sister, Mary, all that we do not yet know." Peter's face betrayed his words. I saw in his face the man who had knelt in the dirt. The stranger with a stone.

I was tired. "Perhaps we can go to my family in Bethany. I do not know when I will see them again once we all set out. Bethany is a safe place." We all lay down about the room. Uneasy, I lay awake for a long time.

I had started to doze, when I heard Peter whisper to someone in the darkness: "Why would Yeshua speak privately with a woman—impart sacred secrets to her—and not openly tell us? Did he prefer her to us? No. Are we to turn about and listen to her? No."

The reply came from Andrew. "The Teacher loved her. He loved us all. But their love is... different. Who are you to reject her?"

Peter's hissed voice sounded like a serpent: "Yeshua called me—he said, 'upon this rock, I will build my church.' It is God's will. Not the woman. Me."

There would be no sleep for me that night—staring up into the dark—wondering how, after coming this far, I would survive among my brothers long enough to teach them what they must know.

Then, turning my head, I saw Yeshua. Sitting beside me.

THE FAMILY AT BETHANY

In the morning, Joseph came to the chamber and we told him of the plan to go to Bethany. He assented, but said, "It would not be safe to all travel together. You are recognizable now and it is not safe—Caiaphas still fears. He sees Yeshua's followers everywhere. He is paranoid and dangerous. If you would see your brother and sister again, I can bring you safely to Bethany and back to Jerusalem in a day."

I was unsure. Martial law had been declared after news of Yeshua's resurrection spread like a fire through the city. But I needed to see Martha and Lazarus—to tell them all that had happened and to prepare them to follow Yeshua—the risen Christ.

Martha ran to meet us—hugging me tight. She did not seem to notice me wince in pain as she grabbed my hand.

"Where is Lazarus?" I asked.

Martha smiled sadly—"In the garden. He is waiting for you." She took my arm and said; "He is different now. He eats so little. Almost never speaks. It is as though there is nothing left to say."

Lazarus. Changed. So frail.

In the brightness of day, it seemed I could almost see through his body.

We embraced and I took care not to hold him too tight. Brushing the hair away from his face, I looked at my beautiful ghost brother. Something there—in his eyes. Perhaps he had not wanted to come back. Had he seen Heaven? Or something else? The answer remained locked in his eyes. I kissed him as softly as I could.

He smiled. "Mary. Come sing to me."

He touched my twisted hands, but did not grasp. He gazed at them.

"I know who you are, Mary." he said softly.

I could not lose him again.

Not staying the night, we gathered provisions. Martha, Lazarus, Joseph and I returned to Jerusalem and the upper chamber.

A RUDDERLESS BOAT

Memories of fear.

Of being so afraid. That stormy night.

Running fast in the dark, urged on through pelting rain by the voices beside me. Running from that safe place where we gathered in the upper chamber. Where I had brought Martha. Lazarus.

Darkness in the room. No lamps lit.

Rain drumming on the roof. Not safe now.

Peter came to me. He told me that some of our "friends"—the hidden faithful in the city who watched out for us—had come to the chamber to warn that our safe place had been discovered. Whether by betrayal or by chance, our arrest was imminent.

Peter said he feared for my safety: "Sister, we know that the Savior loved you more than the rest of us. You must be kept safe. Go away from here for a time." I was startled—how could I leave without giving them what I knew they needed to hear?" Peter insisted. It was just for the immediate time—until martial law was lifted.

My family and I must be preserved—safely smuggled out of the city.

My family. Martha. Lazarus. It was my love for them—my instinct to keep them from harm—that stopped me from hesitating. Peter said he had provisions at the ready and a ship waiting in the port. We must follow him. We must leave. Now.

Joseph, Martha, Lazarus and I followed Peter through the back alleys toward the port. No one seemed to notice us as we spirited past dimly lit windows. It was as if the whole city knew and did not wish to see what was happening. When we reached the port, I gasped aloud. The ship seemed so small. Frail. Like an ancient, shriveled old man.

Joseph protested but Peter urged us aboard— Pilate's men were coming—he had caught sight of them. We would sail southward to Egypt, he said, and send word back with this ship's captain. Soon, the rest would come to join us. We would all be together. Peter lifted Lazarus up to Joseph's waiting arms. Lazarus could not climb the rope ladder by himself.

My beautiful shadow brother. So changed. Not dead, but not really alive, either—no longer fully present in this world for having seen beyond.

Peter spoke to the ship's master and handed him a small bag. The master and his men hauled in the lines and opened the raised sail. We were immediately moving—sudden and forceful—like falling. We steered outward and away from the shore—southward, lurching up and down on the waves. None of us seemed to be breathing. Soon, I saw Peter, coming from the bow of the ship. His face ecstatic—possessed—his eyes wild. He was shouting—there were soldiers! Soldiers on the ship, below deck in the hold—someone had betrayed us! We must all get down into the smaller boat that was lashed to the ship's hull before the soldiers came above. Huddle down and hide within it. It was growing calm. The storm would pass.

We would escape in the smaller boat during the night.

"Certainly, we have endured other storms," Peter said.

Memories of fear. I recalled crossing over the sea of Galilee—Yeshua appearing to us on the rolling waves. He told us "Do not be afraid." Then to Peter, he said: Go into the water." Peter climbed over the side and stood on... nothing. A miracle. Then—he panicked. As his faith fled, he sank under the surface. We hauled him back into the boat. Yeshua calmed the storm and we crossed safely in to Galilee. Where was Peter's faith now? Or my own?

"Quickly!" Peter said.

No time for me to ask, "Then what? Once the storm eased and we were adrift in that small boat—then what?"

"Quickly, Mary!" Peter shoved a small sack into my arms and hoisted me up over the hull and into the little boat. I stowed the sack low and wedged it into the bow. I turned and lifted my arms to receive... no one. I heard voices and strained to see in the falling darkness. No one.

I tried to climb back toward the deck above. Peter rushed at me with a knife in his hand. "Peter! Where are the others? Are the soldiers coming?" He took me by the throat: "No soldiers, treacherous woman—I do not need soldiers to be rid of you—false, tempting prophet!"

He pushed me back into the small boat, cut the tie lines and shoved outward. I did not have time to scream that we had been deceived. The boat lurched free—falling from its attachments and down into the sea. All black.

I fell. As the little boat rose and plunged, I curled myself down, tightly shoved into the narrow bow, my body wrapped around the sack there. Clinging to its weight. I could do nothing. I couldn't move from that spot.

Minutes? Hours? How much lurching, sickening time was passing?

Eloi, Eloi, lama sabachthani?

I shut my eyes tight. I thought of him. Quieting the storm.

Waiting for me on a peaceful shore.

"Help me Rabboni, help me."

I don't know if I fell into a faint. Everything went dark. I felt a great expansion in my chest. And I heard it—Yeshua's voice:

"Mary. Where do you think I am now? Is God's kingdom not within you?

"Magdalene. Command this storm to stop."

I opened my eyes into the brightness of day.

Calm.

Blinking in the sunlight, I looked around me and saw...

Nothing.

Water.

Water! I was burning with thirst—scrambling for the sack—was it still with me? Yes! And within—a sealed jar of clean water. I drank. It hit my empty, tortured stomach like a stone. I tore through the sack to see what food there might be.

I found five loaves and two fishes.

Peter.

Without humor, but not without a sense of irony.

That night, I slept, and drifted into this vision: Yeshua and I were once again sitting by a fire on the familiar hills near Jerusalem. I was writing in the scroll and Yeshua was speaking.

"I am seen by the faithful as being with them on a slave ship, veering far off course under an oppressive master whose name is Ignorance.

"Their faith tells them I am the mutineer that will free them.

"When the mutineer is made the master, the ship will be righted."

In the morning, I reached into the sack and tore a bit of bread. Wet and mildewy, but food. Grabbing a fish, I could smell early decay. Its taste in my mouth was a terrible tang. I could not swallow. Hanging over the side of the boat, I spat into the endless water. I wept. I was hungry. I was sick. Tears became cries. Cries became wails. Wails became screams and those screams became a kind of hysterical laughing bark. I could hardly breathe. I half lay—half fell—on to the floor of the boat, feeling water with my hand. Leaky. A leaky, rudderless, sail-less boat.

The sun blazed down from the empty sky.

I stared at it. Waiting for it to burn me to death. A strange noise—tiny, far away bells—as I stared, the sun seemed to swell and turn bright white.

A host of angels swimming in the air. "Breathe. "Magdalene. Do not be afraid Go into the water."

Breathe. I struggled to pull my body over the side.

Darkness. Suffocating. Not being able to surface. Pushing forward in the black—pushing forward— lungs exploding-pushing, pushing. Gone.

I was awakened by the pain in my body, thudding up and down on the stones of the shore. My legs would not hold me. I wriggled my way a few feet to the moist sand and slept. That is how I came to this place.

MAXIMIN OF GAUL

Beautiful.

A wholly unfamiliar place. Large birds, pink and comical in appearance—and above the shore—the green of a grassy meadow.

A small stone dwelling. I closed my eyes. Opened them again. Still there. Not a dream. Rising, I walked slowly—every bone and muscle creaking and popping in protest.

Making it to the door of the dwelling, I knocked, and a voice answered.

"Who is there?"

"Let me in, in the name of the Lord."

And the door was opened to me by a stranger who would become an old friend.

He brought me to his table and then did a remarkable thing: He brought a basin of water and washed my feet.

He brought bread and wine to the table and offered prayer, saying, "We do this in remembrance of Him."

I stared. "Where are we?"

"This is Gaul, Sister. I am your servant. I am called Maximin."

I asked him who he was remembering with the bread and wine.

He told me of the sacrifice of a great prophet—a messiah, who had been born in Israel to reclaim God's people. To forgive sin and bring about the kingdom of heaven.

Here! So far away! Had I been drifting on that boat for decades? How was this known in Gaul? He told me there were many Jews in Gaul. Some of them came only a short time ago, proclaiming the news of Yeshua's mission. They had come here to escape persecution for their new faith. Maximin himself had been to Jerusalem many times in his life—Gaul was a sort of sanctuary for expatriates from Judea and passage to Jerusalem was easy to arrange.

He had heard Yeshua teach in Jerusalem! I was dumbfounded.

'Sister, what are you called?"

I hesitated for a moment. Who was I now?

"I am called Magdalene."

He started and became very still. Stared. Then he went to his own hearth and, bringing a small alabaster jar, poured its contents out over my feet.

"I know you."

So far away—I had at last arrived home.

I fell into a swoon and slept. After that day, I spent life traveling into Gaul with Maximin at my side, spreading Yeshua's teaching, tending to the afflicted and even baptizing Yeshua's followers into their new lives. I felt such joy. Light.

Connected to the earth and to heaven. Away from the Temple's oppressive presence, away from Peter's fear and doubt—and his threats. I was exhilarated.

One day, Maximin asked, "What do you carry with you?"

Looking down where he pointed, I was surprised to see that I still had the leather pouch at my waist—it had not been lost or destroyed in the sea, but it had been forgotten. Become an appendage—simply accepted and not noticed. I took the scroll from the pouch and offered it to Maximin, for he could read and write. He seemed to devour it—it was as if it were food and he a starving man. It had grown late and the candles were almost spent when he finally looked up and said, "Teacher—it is not finished."

And I knew.

I had to finish the scroll.

I had to record the truth Yeshua had imparted only to me.

I had never shared it. I had held it inside myself—waiting, I suppose, for the time to be right for one of my apostles to come.

Waiting for a sign.

Here was my sign.

Here was my apostle, saying:

"Teacher, it is not finished."

That night, alone outside the cottage, I felt him next to me. Opening my eyes, I saw Yeshua. He held open his hands and smiled at me.

A brilliant but soft light surrounded him. I felt myself expanding.

He rose up slowly and seemed to dissolve as he went. Becoming part of the air. The Spirit. Then he was gone.

I made ready to leave. I would go up in to the rocks above the shoreline where I had landed. There, I would recall all that I had witnessed. All that I knew to be Truth. From that moment until this day, I have not spoken to any living person. Maximin brings me ink made from plants, leaving it at the mouth of the cave. We do not meet.

My days have all been the same.

I pray.

In the sacred silence, I pray to let go—to become unattached to earthly concerns. To be freed of that which holds me down. Fear. Ignorance.

I am again with Yeshua. The kingdom within.

And I remember. I offer these memories to the Lord and I scratch them down on to the grainy surface of the scroll. I have not slept, but my dreams have been vivid—each moment of my life with Yeshua—each word. Each instant so real.

I have been blessed with the gift of living my life over again.

Some moments joyful. Some beyond agony. It has taken me these thirty years to re-live each experience and capture it in words. To witness for all people now and all the people to come.

After a time, my hands even stopped hurting. I do not remember the last time I ate food. Was it all that time ago—next to Maximin's hearth? How strange. I cannot truly feel my body. No physical pain. No hunger. No thirst. I feel a joyful, living peace—like there is a quiet breeze gently blowing through me.

These words I have written that you have not yet heard are what you must know. Those who have ears, let them hear—meditate on these truths—absorb them into yourself, for they are absolute.

My infinite joy of becoming is now only singular, but it is meant for all.

You are called.

Not from above, but from within.

So much more than a question of "sin"—of right or wrong.

Yeshua calls upon you to become fully human.

Both male and female, both dark and light, both flesh and spirit.

All at once.

Yeshua said: "Listen to me: Two parts of one spirit."

That is not just him and me. That is man and God.

We are not separate from God. This is the great truth that has been lost to humankind.

You must find that truth again. The kingdom of God is within you.

Therefore, love the Lord your God with all your heart and with all your soul and with all your mind. This is the first and greatest commandment. And the second is like it: Love your neighbor as yourself.

It is so very simple.

Perhaps that is why it is so difficult. This morning, Maximin came to leave ink.

For the first time in a very long time, I went to meet him.

I must have appeared very different this morning. He was startled and dropped the jar of ink. We watched the dark liquid flow into the dirt, just as I had watched precious spikenard flow into the dust of an empty tomb so long ago. I led him to this spot—where I stand now.

And this small jar—I gave it to him. He knew.

He opened the jar. Poured its fragrant balm over my head.

No words uttered. I kissed his hands and he left me.

He will return—when I am gone.

Become spirit. Become whole. Reunited.

When Maximin comes next, he will find an empty body.

And he will find the scroll.

With this, Maximin will travel.

To Rome.

He will bring this to my brother.

Peter.

He and Paul have been sharing Yeshua's teachings there.

In Rome.

The empire itself.

I do not know what became of John or Matthew or James—or any of my brothers.

Joseph the Sanhedrin.

Martha.

Lazarus.

I do know that my work is done.

Yeshua came to me.

"Prepare," he said.

So.

Peter will have my scroll.

Because Peter must have my scroll.

It is as it should be.

Peter will know the truth.

He will have all that he needs to build his church.

To build his church.

Upon this rock.

My testament.

The gospel of Mary, the Magdalene.

It is finished.

ROXANNE FAY is an actor and writer. Formerly the Producing Artistic Director for the Oak Park Festival Theatre in Chicago, she now resides in the Tampa Bay area of Florida and serves as Producing Artistic Director for Circle In The Water, LLC. She is the first recipient of the Jeff Norton Dream Grant, awarded by Theatre Tampa Bay to fund the creation of her new play, *Upon This Rock: The Magdalene Speaks* (based on her book of the same name), which premiered May 27, 2014. Her collected plays, *Home Fires Burning*, were presented at St. Petersburg, Florida's Studio@620, where she is an Associate Artist. She has received awards in Florida for her work in productions of *Cabaret, Much Ado About Nothing*, and *Side Man*.

www.roxannefay.com and
www.circleinthewater.com

29966956R00070

Made in the USA
Charleston, SC
31 May 2014